To my mom, who read to me.
And to my dad, who let me choose any book I wanted. —R.C.

For the books that I devoured and to the family that fed my obsession,
thank you for wrapping me up in your stories. —M.C.

Text copyright © 2018 by Rachael Cole

Jacket art and interior illustrations copyright © 2018 by Melissa Crowton

All rights reserved. Published in the United States by Schwartz & Wade Books, an imprint of Random House Children's Books,
a division of Penguin Random House LLC, New York.

Schwartz & Wade Books and the colophon are trademarks of Penguin Random House LLC.

Visit us on the Web! rhcbooks.com

Educators and librarians, for a variety of teaching tools, visit us at RHTeachersLibrarians.com

Library of Congress Cataloging-in-Publication Data
Names: Cole, Rachael, author. | Crowton, Melissa, illustrator.
Title: Mousie, I will read to you / Rachael Cole ; illustrated by Melissa Crowton.
Description: First edition. | New York : Schwartz & Wade Books, [2018]
Summary: "Follows a mama mouse and her baby mouse on the little mouse's journey to becoming a reader—
from infancy to toddlerhood to elementary school and beyond"—Provided by publisher.
Identifiers: LCCN 2017043724 (print) | LCCN 2017057098 (ebook) | ISBN 978-1-5247-1538-0 (ebook)
ISBN 978-1-5247-1536-6 (hardcover) | ISBN 978-1-5247-1537-3 (library binding)
Subjects: | CYAC: Books and reading—Fiction. | Mother and child—Fiction. | Growth—Fiction. | Mice—Fiction.
Classification: LCC PZ7.1.C643 (ebook) | LCC PZ7.1.C643 Mou 2018 (print) | DDC [E]—dc23

The text of this book is set in 19-point Kepler.

The illustrations in this book were rendered digitally.

MANUFACTURED IN CHINA

2 4 6 8 10 9 7 5 3 1

First Edition

MOUSIE, I WILL READ TO YOU

WRITTEN BY

RACHAEL COLE

ILLUSTRATED BY

MELISSA CROWTON

schwartz & wade books · new york

Long before the words make sense, Mousie,

I will read to you

The simplest story

About an acorn that drops to the ground.

While we are rocking,

I will whisper in your ear

A sentence

About a soft rain coming down.

When summer comes,

And you are tired from swinging on the swings,

I will sing you

A lullaby

About the sun fading slowly

While the sky fills with stars.

In the middle of the night,

When your crying fills the room,

I will read you

A poem

About the quietest forest,

Where the only sounds are the crickets,

Whispering *sh-Sha sh-Sha*

Just for you.

When morning comes,

I will fill your listening ears with words

About sun drying dew off the grass

And clearing away the cold and dark of night.

Before you know it, Mousie,

Your DAA DAA DEEs and BAA BAA BEEs

sound like jazz.

I will answer back as you smile,

With words that echo yours,

Like DADDY and BUMBLEBEE.

Your first words fall out of your mouth like treasures—

DADA, BABY, BYE-BYE.

I will scoop them up

And write them down.

Soon after you turn two,

On a foggy neighborhood walk,

You tell me, "There! A tree!"

And I will answer, "It's a strong oak.

The squirrels love to play in it."

After bathtime, cozy in pajamas,

You'll climb into my lap,

Asking for the book about the bear.

The day falls away.

It's just you

And me,

And the rhythm of the words.

I will take you to a library near a playground.

And now that you're a big boy,

You will pick out your own book.

And while sitting on a bench outside,

You will surprise me by reading a word.

Then two,

Then three.

Years later,

I will find you,

With a flashlight in your room,

Reading a chapter book

To your stuffed animals.

I will quietly close the door

And leave you be.

And when you are grown,

You will read about things

I've never known

And haven't dared to dream.

Then one day, before you know it,

On a blanket in a forest,

You will read a story

To *your* baby . . .

. . . about an acorn that drops to the ground.